J.C. HULSEY BOOKS

REBECCA

J.C. HULSEY

When she saw the tall dark man with the flint-colored eyes, she felt a flutter in her mid-section. What was it about him that affected her so? She stared at his mouth, wondering if his lips would feel as soft as they looked. When he told his partner to go on without him, she again felt something churn her insides. Then he turned around, walked toward her and stopped in front of her. When he spoke, his voice commanded that she obey, which she would do gladly. Is there such a thing as love at first sight? She believed there was, because she was in love, with this stranger.

He was an outlaw, a robber and a thief.

When he saw the effect the woman had on the other men, he thought they were being foolish, but then he took a second look and he felt his heart start to race and was having a hard time breathing.

What could this frightened freckled face redhead with the piercing green eyes have that is so different from all the other women he had known?

Love at first sight is a myth, or is it?

CHAPTER ONE

Her pale green eyes had a frightened look as she stared straight ahead. The breeze was blowing her long red hair across her face almost covering her freckles. She was young wearing a plain blue and white dress which failed to hide her full figure. She held a small carpet bag tightly in her tiny hands. Every man stared at her in awe. They stopped in their tracks and looked at her as though she was a figment of their imagination. It seemed I was the only one who escaped her hypnotic effect. I shoved Virgil and got his attention.

I had been the leader of this gang of ragtag rejects for going on six months. We were all a bunch of misfits that would rather hold up a stage or a bank than look at the rear end of a cow all day. Virgil was my second in command, but lately he had been questioning my decisions.

One good thing about our gang, if there is anything good about a bunch of thieves, is we're not killers. The reason for that is my daddy was a sheriff when I was a kid. He died trying to stop a bank robbery.

I know how Ma and me felt when he didn't come home that day. I don't want to be responsible for some wife or kid crying because their loved one didn't come home.

"What's the matter with you? We got a job to do. Now get on with it." I yelled at Virgil.

He jumped into action hollering at the other men and grabbed the strongbox from under the seat.

"Whoo hoo! We're gonna be rich." He loaded the box onto the pack horse that we had brought with us.

"Alright. Virgil, mount up and let's get outta here."

I took another look at the young lady. She had silver-colored tears sliding down her cheeks. Suddenly it hit me. I was going to take her with me.

"You boys go ahead; I'll catch up to you. Should be there before dark."

"What're you gonna do? Asked Virgil."

"I said I'd catch up. Now move out."

He reluctantly turned and headed out behind the others. I got outta the saddle and walked to the girl.

I stepped in front of her. She lifted her head and my breath left my body when those piercing green eyes locked with mine. I felt as if she was looking straight into my soul. I could feel her drawing me into her world with just a look.

I glanced at the other passengers, then back at her.

"This your only bag?" I asked.

She nodded.

"You got something in there fit for riding?"

She nodded again.

"Put it on, you're going with me." She turned and went behind the stagecoach.

One of the passengers, a plump elderly woman with a shrill voice who didn't seem to mind using it yelled, "You can't take her!"

"She can stay if she wants to," I told her.

She returned shortly wearing a man's outfit. It only accentuated her curves. I helped her into the saddle.

"Move your foot so's I can get up behind you." I slid my boot into the stirrup and swung up behind her. The top of her head rested under my chin. I inhaled deeply.

It's been too long, I thought.

She twisted, trying to adjust to the saddle. I felt the closeness of her and inhaled again.

"You hungry? I asked.

She nodded.

"It's not much further. We'll stop up ahead."

We stopped in a little draw, dismounted and drank from the canteen.

"Here's some jerky. It's a little hard to chew, but if you'll let it soak in your mouth, it'll soften enough you can chew and swallow it.

"I need to go behind these bushes first," she said as she disappeared behind them.

I sat with my back against the tree watching her as she walked back from the bushes. She was really something to look at.

I started thinking to myself. *Do I really want to go back to the hideout with her and face the boys? I saw the way they looked at her. Maybe it'd be better to head to Flanagan's place. It's not but ten more miles or so. That's what we'll do.*

Albert McGrue Flanagan's a chubby fellow with a round face. It always seems to be flushed as if he's just finished a foot race. He's young to be the owner of a large Ranch like The Circle Four, but he is. Some say he won it in a poker game. Others say he inherited it from an uncle. I was probably the only one that knew the truth.

He and I had been a member of the famous Henderson Gang. We were the only survivors of a bank holdup. Every member of the gang was killed as they left the scene. Flanagan and I slipped out the back door and got away with forty thousand dollars. He came to Rockford, Texas and bought the Ranch from an elderly gent that was ready to retire. He became a respected man in the community. He offered me half interest in the ranch, but I wasn't ready to settle down. Now, however, I might be ready. My ma always told me, when I asked her, how she knew she loved Pa, said when it happens to you, it'll become very clear to you.

She leaned back against me and I tightened my arms around her. She felt good that way. She filled an emptiness deep inside me. I had known a lot of girls, but none of them ever had this effect on me. As we drew closer to Flanagan's I began to think that I didn't want to share her with him either. *Why would I feel this way about Flanagan? He'd never do anything to hurt me. But he is a man. I remember how the boys looked at her back at the stage. I've got to stop being this way. We can't stay away from people all the time. I've never been this taken with a woman before. What is it about her? Sure, she's very good looking, but there's something else. I reckon I ain't no better than the boys. She's cast some sort of spell on me, and I don't even know her name.*

CHAPTER TWO

The sun had just disappeared behind the mountain top.

"We're almost there." I told her.

She smelled so good leaning back against me, I wanted to stay this way forever. I stopped my horse at the barn, looking toward the house. There wasn't any movement. Normally, Flanagan would be running out to meet me.

I helped her off the horse. She staggered a little falling back against me. I helped her stand again, not wanting to let her go.

"You wait here, I need to check the house." I walked to the front door, watching for any movement anywhere. I reached out to knock on the door when I heard something. I opened the door and stepped inside. Flanagan was lying on the floor. Looked like he'd been shot. I rushed to his side, cradling his head in my lap.

"I'm sure glad to see you." he mumbled.

"What happened?" I asked him.

He mumbled something I couldn't understand. I let his head down easy and went to the door to call her inside. I stepped outside and motioned for her to come in.

She started walking toward me and I couldn't take my eyes off her swaying figure. The way her full hips filled out those trousers was kind of hypnotizing.

I turned away and went back to Flanagan. He wasn't making any sound. I knelt beside him and felt for a pulse. He was gone.

She stepped through the door and gasped. "Was he a friend of yours?"

"A very good friend. I'm gonna miss him."

"I'm so sorry," she said. "I'll look for a blanket to cover him." She went into the bedroom and came back carrying a blanket. She handed it to me and I covered him.

"Thank you, that was very thoughtful of you. What's your name?"

"Rebecca."

"Rebecca? You got a last name?"

"I don't think a last name is necessary in this situation, do you?"

I stood. "I'm going to the barn and get a shovel to bury him. You be alright here?"

"I'll be fine. You want me to make something to eat?"

"Sure, that would be great. I'll be back shortly." I found a shovel and buried Albert McGrue Flanagan under the big tree that he liked so much. I went back inside and it the food smelled swell.

"I found some things for a meal. I hope you like it."

"I'm sure it'll be fine. How come you came with me?"

"I don't know, why did you take me?"

"I wish I could answer that. It seemed like the right thing to do at the time. You got a family? Anybody that's gonna miss you?"

"I was on my way to meet my finance. I don't think I'm going to make it, do you?"

"Not unless you want to. I'll take you back if that's what you want."

"I don't want to go back; I like where I'm at."

"I ain't never done nothing like this before."

"Me neither."

"My name's Yancy Calhoun."

"Pleased to meet you, Yancy Calhoun. Come, sit and eat before it gets cold."

I don't think I've ever tasted a better meal, than what she placed in front of me. It wasn't anything special, but I thought it was because she made it.

"You're staring at me."

"I'm sorry, but I can't help myself. This has never happened to me before."

"Me neither. What are we going to do?"

"What do you want to do?"

"Let's just take it one step at a time. How's that sound to you? How long are you planning on staying here?"

"I don't have any plans in mind. Would you like to stay here for a while?"

"I think I'd like that."

"That was delicious. Thank you for making it."

"Was this your friend's place?"

"Yes, he's been here for about five years. He's going to be missed. He was a good friend."

"Would it be possible for me to take a bath? I really need to wash off this dust and grime."

"There should be a tub around here someplace. You should start heating water. I'll carry in more as soon as I locate the tub."

I found the tub next to the back door. I brought it in and set it in the middle of the room. She already had water heating on the stove. I grabbed the bucket and headed to the well in the back yard. I carried seven buckets in for her. It took almost three hours to heat enough hot water.

When the tub was filled with water, she looked at me and asked, "Do you want to join me?"

"Are you kidding me? Of course I want to join you."

She began removing her riding clothes. I could hardly believe what I was seeing. An angel sent down from heaven couldn't have been any more beautiful. She stepped into the tub and sat down.

"Well, what are you waiting for?"

"Just enjoying the view." I had my clothes off in record time. I stepped in behind her, thankful that this was a full-sized tub. I sat with my legs on both sides of her. She leaned her head back against me.

"This is a wonderful feeling, isn't it?"

"Couldn't be any better." I picked up a cloth that was laying on the floor and began washing her back.

"Hmm. Even better. Wash in front." I was in heaven. This was a special woman. I was in a tub with her and she had just asked me to wash her front. I touched her in unspeakable places with that wet cloth.

"Let me do you? We need to stand up and turn around." She stood and turned. I stood facing her.

"Are you going to turn around?" I reluctantly turned my back to her. When her hand touched my skin, I thought I had died and gone to heaven.

"Alright, time to get out." We stepped out together. She picked up two towels, handing me one. She started drying me. I mimicked her every movement. She indicated I should turn. I did so, dreading it.

She tapped me on the shoulder. "My turn." I turned and saw her back. A more beautiful sight I had never seen. When she was dry, she leaned into me.

"Now that I'm clean, I believe I'm ready for bed. How about you?"

"I'm ready."

She headed for the bedroom with me right behind her. She turned the covers down and slipped into bed. I lost no time climbing in beside her. She held out her arms, inviting me to hold her. Her skin was like velvet. Smooth and warm and she smelled like a woman. I placed my lips against hers. She inhaled slightly and her lips opened to allow entrance. What a marvelous feeling. Her hand moved lower and touched a place that hadn't been touched for quite some time.

"You need to slow down if you expect me to reciprocate. She pulled her hand back. "I didn't mean for you to stop. Just slow down a bit."

We continued deep kissing and hugging.

"I'm ready if you are," she said.

 "Oh yes." I positioned myself above her. She moaned. I didn't last long.

"I'm sorry, if we wait a little bit, I should be able to satisfy you."

"I'm very satisfied," she said.

Is this a real woman? It was the most wonderful night I've ever had in my entire life. The next morning came absolutely too soon. I turned to see her, but she wasn't there. I immediately had a bad feeling. *What would I do if she decided to leave? I had just found the most wonderful woman in the world. She can't be gone.* I quickly got out of bed and dressed. I walked into the other room and there she was standing at the stove turning strips of bacon. I took a deep breath, relieved that she was still here. She was dressed in the same dress she was wearing on the stagecoach.

"Good morning." she said turning to look at me. The sunlight shining through the window accentuated her freckles which I thought made her even more beautiful. "Breakfast is almost ready. You need to run outside first?"

"Yeah, I reckon I better." I hurried back inside as she was placing a platter on the table. "Smells great."

"See if it tastes the same?"

"Umm, it's delicious." as I shoveled eggs in my mouth.

CHAPTER THREE

We stayed at Flanagan's place for almost a month. The days were long with nothing to do, but walk around the place looking at the animals and strolling in the meadow. The nights were a different story. They were filled with passion, companionship and, yes, love.

We often talked afterwards, deep into the night. She told me her fiancé would probably send someone to look for her. He had struck a bargain with one of his closest friends, Albert Gilstrap, the banker in their small town, for her to marry him. She tried to talk her father out of it, but he said he owed the bank a large sum of money, and this was the only way to settle his debt. His friend had been eyeing her since she was very young.

"I was glad when you came along. You might say you're my hero. You rescued me from a fate worse than death. He's a dirty man as old as my father, and I didn't want to marry him."

"There's no reason we can't stay here indefinitely. Flanagan always said that half the ranch belonged to me. He also told me where he hid the rest of the money in case anything ever happened to him. Which brings up something else. Who killed him and why?"

"Do you think they might come back?"

"I don't know. If they were looking for something and didn't find it, yes, they might come back and search some more. Are you worried that I can't protect you?"

"That's not it at all. I'm worried that something might happen to you."

"I've been taking care of myself for quite a few years."

"That was before you had me to worry about. I'm afraid you might be so concerned about me that you'll put yourself in harm's way."

"They might not even come back. Let's not worry until it happens."

"It might be too late to worry then."

"We're gonna be alright, I promise. Now come here."

"I'm gonna go into town and get supplies. Do you want to come along, or do you want to stay here?"

"I think I'll go with you in case Flanagan's killers decide to come back. Is that alright with you?"

"I asked, didn't I? Let me go hook up the buckboard. I think it'll be easier on you than riding, in front of me, on my horse."

"I didn't mind that a bit. In fact, I liked it. How far is it into town?"

"'Bout ten miles. Should take a little more than two hours. I'll give a holler when I'm ready."

"I'll be ready."

I went to the corral, picked out the horses for the wagon and hooked them up. I glanced up and spotted two horses in the distance. I checked my sidearm to make sure I was ready for trouble. I strolled back to the house and stepped inside.

"Who is it? Can you see who it is?"

"Not yet. You stay outa sight until I find out what they want."

"Be careful, Yancy, please."

"I will."

I grabbed the carbine setting by the door and stepped back outside. As the riders got closer, I recognized one of them. It was Virgil.

"Lookee here. If it ain't old Yancy Calhoun. What'cha doing out here? You never did come to the hideout like you said. The boys divvied up the money amongst themselves. They said if you had a problem with it, you knew where to find them."

"What are you doing here, Virgil?"

"Mr. Gilstrap, here, hired me to help him find his fiancé. Said she was on a certain stagecoach. I think you know which one I'm talking about. Said she was a redhead. You haven't seen a redhead, have you, Yancy?"

"No. I haven't seen anybody like that. When did you hire out to hunt people?"

"It's easy money. Not any danger. Not like some professions."

"Like I said. Ain't seen nobody like that around here. Now if you'll excuse me, I've got some things to take care of."

Virgil narrowed his eyes and said, "You sure you ain't seen a redheaded woman? The passengers on the stage said a man looked something like you carried her off."

"I done told you I ain't seen nobody."

"Would you mind if I took a look around?"

"I would. I would recommend you and this gentleman should ride on down the trail."

"Sure thing, Yancy. Maybe we'll see you later?"

They turned their mounts and went back the way they rode in. I watched until I couldn't see them. I went back inside.

"You find out who they were? What they want?"

"It was a friend of mine and your fiancé. They were looking for a redheaded woman. I told them there wasn't anyone like that around here."

"Thank you. I was so scared. You could have been hurt. Why did you just walk out and confront them like that?"

"The only way to face trouble is face to face. Besides one of them was Virgil. He's a friend. Or he was."

"We still going to town?"

"We need supplies. Maybe you should consider staying here. If Virgil and his friend are there, it would be dangerous. If you stay out of sight you should be okay."

"If that's what you think. I can hide if I see someone."

"I think that would be best. I'll be back as soon as I can. I'm leaving my rifle for you, just in case. You can use a rifle, can't you?

"Of course, I've been shooting ever since I was very young."

"Goodbye, darling."

"Goodbye."

I took her in my arms. She tilted her head up. I kissed her with every ounce of feeling in my body.

CHAPTER FOUR

I walked to the wagon, climbed aboard and headed in the direction of town. I had only been on the trail for a short time when I heard gunfire. I pulled up on the reins, turning the wagon and headed back to the ranch. I pulled into the yard and jumped down. Virgil was laying on the ground. He wasn't moving.

"Rebecca! I don't want to hurt you. I love you. Put the gun down and come out." Gilstrap said loudly.

Rebecca responded with another shot which came awfully close to the banker's head.

"Yancy? Is that you?" she asked.

"It's me. You sit tight. I'll take care of Mr. Gilstrap. Gilstrap? You hear me?"

"I hear you. This ain't no concern of yours. Stay outa it," he answered.

"Can't do that. She belongs to me. Best thing for you to do is mount up and ride out. Otherwise, you'll be joining Virgil. If it was me, I'd ride out," he shouted at me.

"What was it you said, can't do that."

"She was promised to me by her father."

"She wasn't his to be promised. She's not a piece of property that can be bought or sold. She's a human being and she is capable of making her own decisions. Now. One last time. Ride out while you're still able."

A slug whizzed by my head. I fell to the ground and threw a shot in his direction.

"Uhh! You shot me. You weren't supposed to shoot me. She's mine."

He slid to the ground looking like a broken doll. I stood, walked to where he had fallen and kicked his pistol away. I bent over and checked his pulse. He was dead.

Rebecca came running from the house, screaming my name.

"Yancy! Yancy! Are you hurt? Are you okay?"

"I'm fine. How about you? They didn't hurt you, did they?"

"No, I'm okay. I heard their horses and remembered what you said about facing trouble head on, so that's what I did. I stepped out with the rifle in my hand, ready to shoot. I even let them have their say. When Albert said he was going to take me back even though I didn't want to go, I raised the gun and shot that man you called Virgil. I'm sorry I shot your friend."

"He wasn't a friend if he was coming for you. I'm just glad you're alright. As soon as I bury this hombre we can go to town. I think it'll be okay for you to come with me now. Will you be ready?"

CHAPTER FIVE

She sat very close to me for the complete trip. We pulled into town around four o'clock. I stopped in front of the general store. Set the brake, looped the reins around the handle and hopped down. I ran around to the other side to help Rebecca down. I held her close as she slid down my body.

"Yancy! People can see us."

"Do you care?"

"Not really, but we should attempt some sort of respectability while we're in town."

I released her, offered my arm and we entered the building. The inside was dark and gloomy as most general stores are.

A tall elderly woman looked up from the counter with tired, but friendly eyes. She brushed a wisp of gray hair back from her forehead with one hand, raising the other in greeting. "Good day to you. Welcome to Hamilton's Mercantile. Is there anything I can help you with?"

"Yes, thank you, ma'am. I have a list here someplace. Aw, yes, here it is." I handed her a crumpled piece of paper.

She straightened it out, perused the list and said, "We got most everythin' on the list except butter. We ain't had no butter ever since Mr. Dobbin's cow died. He said he wus gonna git another one, but he ain't done it yet. You and the missus wanna take a stroll around town while I fill this? Gonna take 'bout half an hour."

"That's an excellent suggestion. Would you like to take a tour of the town, darling?"

"Sounds marvelous, darling."

She slid her arm into mine and we exited the store, turning left on the sidewalk.

The sky was a clear blue with just a hint of puffy white clouds. A slight north breeze was whipping around the corner of the buildings, a welcome relief to the July heat.

We stopped at several windows to look at the goods.

"Oh my. Isn't that a lovely dress? And it looks to be my size. Can we go in and let me try it on?" The dress was yellow with blue flower patterns on it. The perfect color for Rebecca's complexion.

"Absolutely. After you my dear." I opened the door and followed her inside.

A middle-aged woman came from a curtain. "Good day to you folks. Are you looking for a dress for the missus?"

"I'd like to look at the dress in the window. Try it on if that's alright?" said Rebecca.

"Of course you may try it on, otherwise you'll not know if it'll fit. Let me fetch it and you come with me.

You may sit in the chair at the front of the shop, young man."

"Yes, ma'am." I walked to the front of the shop and sat down in a cane back chair. It wasn't very comfortable. I tried leaning it back, but it was so straight it wouldn't lean.

Rebecca came through the curtain wearing the dress from the window. She was absolutely the most beautiful woman I had ever laid eyes on.

The dress fit as if it was made specifically for her. The color was perfect for her flaming red hair and green eyes.

"Do you like it?" she asked. "I mean really like it."

"You're beautiful." I replied.

"I love it, but I don't have any money. Do you...?"

"Don't worry about money. If you want it, it's yours. I'll take care of it."

She put her arms around my neck, pulled me down and gave me one of our special kisses.

"We're in a public place, remember?" I teased.

"I simply don't care. I love you." She kissed me again.

We had never mentioned the word love in all the times we had been together. But she did say it. She said she loved me.

That word makes this a horse of a different color. Love. That's serious stuff. Do I feel the same? Do I love her?

I think I do, but am I ready to commit to a lifetime relationship? With a woman like Rebecca? Yes. Yes.

"It's time to get back to the store. You ready?" I asked her.

"I'm ready. Thank you so much, Mrs. …. I'm sorry, I don't know your name."

"Hannah Burton. Widow Hannah Burton. I so glad you like the dress. I made it especially for a young person who was going to be married, but the day before the wedding, her fiancé was killed, by some bank robbers. Poor child."

"I'm mighty sorry, ma'am, for your loss and for that poor girl. How much I owe for the dress?"

"Three dollars. I'm letting it go for a discounted price, because I can see how much your wife likes it."

I didn't bother to correct her. It sounded good to my ears.

We walked back to the general store and went inside. Two cowboys, obviously drunk, were fussing with Mrs. Hamilton.

The one doing the talking was a big brute of a man with stubble on his square face, dressed in dungarees and a blue work shirt. The smaller man was clean shaven with cool brown eyes. He looked as if he wanted no part of this confrontation.

"I done told you boys, we ain't got none of that," said Mrs. Hamilton.

"Are you sure, ma'am? What'cha you got in the back room? I think we orta go back and take a look. Don't you think so, Kevin?"

"The back room is off limits to customers, Ringo. You know that," exclaimed Mrs. Hamilton.

"Well, since we ain't bought nothing yet, I don't reckon we're customers. Come on Kev."

"You can't go back there," exclaimed Mrs. Hamilton as she stepped in front of him.

The bigger one pushed her aside and proceeded to push the curtain aside.

"I think you boys should leave." I said calmly, resting my hand on my pistol.

"This don't involve you, mister. You and the young lady need to exit the way you came in, so's nobody gets hurt," the man said.

"You step back outside, please Rebecca. I have to take care of this little problem."

"Some'in' wrong with your hearing, mister?" the man asked.

"I hear just fine. I do believe though that you're the one confused."

"How am I confused?"

"I made a request for you two characters to leave. You haven't done that yet. Now, I'll give you two choices."

"What you mean? Two choices?"

"You can walk out, or you can be carried out. Your choice."

"Kevin, you move over to the right. He can't git both of us."

"But, what if I'm the one he gits? I ain't ready to die over a box of cigars. No thank you. I'll be walking out like the man said," exclaimed Kevin.

"You a coward, Kevin Conroy. I thought we's friends?"

"We are, and as your friend I'm asking you to let this go and come with me."

"Time's a wasting, boys. Make your choice. NOW!" I challenged.

"I didn't want no smokes no how." He turned and headed out the door behind his partner.

"There's one thing you forgot, friend."

"I didn't forget nothing. I'm leaving like you asked."

"You need to apologize to Mrs. Hamilton for the disturbance."

"You're pushing me awful hard, mister. I apologize, ma'am, for me and my friend." He left through the door.

"Thank you, mister. Those boys aren't bad. They just had a little too much to drink. If they had been sober, this wouldn't have happened. I have your supplies ready. My boy ain't here, right now, but I expect him any minute now."

"I believe I'll be able to handle it myself, but thank you for your concern."

"I was so frightened for you, Yancy," said Rebecca.

"It was nothing to worry about. They were a couple of drunk cowboys, that's all. You worry too much, I told her."

"Here's my boy now," said Mrs. Hamilton. As a young man of about 16 came through the curtain.

"Rudy, help these folks load their supplies."

"Yes, Ma," he replied.

Rudy was a gangly kid with a bowl haircut, wearing an apron. He seemed quite taken with Rebecca. I caught him more than once glancing at her. It didn't seem to matter to him that she was with me. She bent over to look at something on the floor, presenting her backside to him. I heard him sigh deeply and swallow real hard. I cleared my throat loudly, he turned, started picking up boxes and carrying them out to the wagon. Rebecca had no idea she had this effect on men.

"Oh look at this, Yancy?" said Rebecca. "It's a riding skirt and blouse. Now I can go riding with you."

I looked at her smiling face and thought to myself. *How can I refuse her anything?*

We got all the supplies loaded, paid Mrs. Hamilton and bid her good day. Rudy was looking around the corner with a lost puppy look on his face.

I hollered, "Rudy! Catch," I tossed a dollar to him. It bounced on the wooden sidewalk and fell through the cracks.

I helped Rebecca up on the seat, climbed up beside her, grabbed the reins, slapped them on the horse's rump, clucked to him, and we headed back to the ranch.

Rebecca starting humming on the ride back. She stopped and asked me, "Do you like music, Yancy?"

"Sure. I like all kinds of music, but I wouldn't try to sing. Sounds like a cow bellowing. You've got a nice voice, though. Keep doing what you're doing. I like it."

CHAPTER SIX

I pulled around to the side of the house, to the door leading into the kitchen. I jumped down, tied the reins to the hitching post and helped Rebecca down.

"You go on. I'll bring all the things in. You can start putting them away."

I don't guess I will ever get tired of watching her walk. The way her hips sway and sort of wiggle.

Even though we had been together for a while now, I was still memorized by her smile and laughter. During the day, when I was away from her, all I could think about was the way she fit in my arms. The way her lips felt when we kissed. I could hardly contain myself enough to complete whatever chore I was doing.

We were relaxing, sitting under the big oak tree when a fancy buggy pulled into the front yard. I told Rebecca to stay out of sight while I found out who it was. I stood and walked toward the arrival.

"How do you do. Are you the owner of this place? I understood when I asked in town that the owner was a short blonde man. It seems you are neither," the man asked

"The owner is unavailable for the time being. Is there something I can help you with?"

"And who are you if I might inquire?"

"I could ask you the same question."

"My name is Horace Olgaby. I'm here inquiring about purchasing this insignificant piece of property."

"And I'm here to tell you it ain't for sell."

"But I was told in town on good authority, the banker in fact, that it was for sell."

"Sometimes folks get mixed up about things. It's not for sell. At any price. Good day to you." With those words I turned and walked away.

I heard Olgaby curse as he turned the buggy back the way he came.

I wondered to myself, *what was all that about? Why would the banker tell Olgaby this place was for sell?*

I left Rebecca at the house while I rode around the ranch to check things out. I wanted to find out why there was no livestock close to the main house.

I came back around suppertime. Rebecca had a meal prepared. She was a wonderful cook. Just another one of her fantastic abilities. She had smothered beef chips, mashed potatoes, green beans and hot biscuits fresh from the oven.

I complimented her on her cooking. "I just want to make you happy. Now wash up and dig in. I want to watch you eat. By the way, do you like pie?"

"You baked a pie too? You're the most wonderful woman in the whole wide world. Thank you."

I was still having difficulty telling her how much I loved her. I didn't doubt my love for her, it was just hard to put it into words.

That night after another wonderful bout of sexual bliss, something kept nagging at me so much I was having a hard time letting sleep overtake me. I was thinking about those dead cows and the visit from Olgaby. Where were the hands? Was Flanagan having trouble of some kind?

I hit my fist on the wall and uttered a curse.

"What's wrong? Did you see something today that upset you? You can tell me."

I grimly confessed to her what I found out on the range.

"Over at the pond, in the south side of the ranch, I found at least fifteen dead cows. Looks as if they had been shot. I followed the trail of the culprits to the fence dividing this place from the neighbors. The trail then headed south to where the gate is located. They went through the gate. I didn't follow any further."

There was something else keeping me from slumber at night. I kept going over and over in my head that first night Rebecca and I made love. At the time I had other things on my mind, but now I realized that I was not her first lover. I could understand my jealousy with the guys in the gang. The way they looked at her at the stage. I was even jealous of Flanagan and he was my best friend.

I had always heard how jealousy could destroy a relationship, but I couldn't help myself. It kept gnawing and gnawing at my insides. I was so worried about it that I knew I was going to have to ask her about it. Would she be truthful, or would she lie? Would I believe her either way? One night after an especially amorous bout of lovemaking I broached the subject.

"Rebecca, I've got something that's been eating at me that needs an answer from you."

"You know you can ask me anything, darling."

"Do you remember our first time?"

"Of course, how could I forget?"

"Normally the first time for a woman is painful. I didn't notice you having any pain. I wasn't your first?"

"Does it really matter to you? Would it make any difference in our lives?"

"It shouldn't, but yes, I need to know."

"Of course you were my first and I'm so glad it was you."

"How come you didn't feel any pain?"

"I can't answer that unless I was so excited and nervous about the situation that I didn't feel anything, but pleasure. I'm so sorry that this is upsetting you this much. Just know this. You were my first and last lover. I promise you that. Do you think you can accept that answer?"

"I'm so sorry for being this way. I just can't think about someone else holding you, touching you the way I do. I'll work on it, but I can't promise that I can change."

CHAPTER SEVEN

"Yancy, come see what I found in the barn this morning?"

"What?"

"Come on, I want you to see for yourself." She grabbed my hand pulling me toward the barn.

"They're back here in this last stall." She guided me to the stall and slightly pushed me in. There, curled up in some hay was a mama cat and six baby kittens.

"Aren't they beautiful?"

"They're adorable."

"I'm going to name each one a very special name.'

I didn't particularly care for felines, but if it made Rebecca happy, I would put up with them.

Rebecca and I sat on the old worn sofa and cuddled. It was a different feeling than I had ever had with any of the other girls I had known. I enjoyed just sitting holding her without talking. She felt so soft and smooth in my arms.

"Why were you robbing the stagecoach? You could have been here, helping Flanagan run the ranch, like he wanted."

"Well, it's this way. I never was very good at work of any kind. Robbing and stealing is a whole lot easier.

Besides, if I hadn't robbed that stage we'd never met. I can promise you that I won't be doing any more robbing now that I've found you. I think this ranch is the perfect place to settle down, especially with someone like you."

"I think I would like that."

"You know there's something about this whole set up that just ain't right. Flanagan told me he kept on all the hands when he bought the old man out. Where are they? By the looks of things, it don't look like any body's been around for quite a spell. Something going on that ain't up to par. I should have asked around town when we were there. Somebody knows something. Maybe I'll go back to town and do some asking. You should be safe here until I get back. Don't you think?"

"Don't worry about me. I can do some baking now that we have supplies. You go ahead. You need to settle this in your mind at least."

The sun was peeking over the horizon, casting its yellow glow over the meadow. I had my horse saddled and ready to ride just as Rebecca came out of the house with a bag in her hand.

"I packed some grub for you. Just some meat between bread slices. Made with a lot of love. You will be careful, won't you?"

"With you here waiting for me. Of course I'll be extra careful. Should be back by sundown. You keep the rifle close. Okay?"

"Don't worry about me. Just hurry home. Doesn't that have a nice ring to it? Home?"

"Sure does." I pulled her into my arms and kissed her deeply. She kissed me back with just as much feeling. I almost changed my mind about going, but I released her, pulled myself into the saddle, winked at her and left at a gallop.

On the ride to town, I thought how my life had changed since I met Rebecca. I had no desire whatsoever to join back with the gang. That life was behind me, just like I told her. Besides, with Virgil dead, the guys have probably spit up and went their own way.

CHAPTER EIGHT

I reached Rockford, Texas around mid-morning. Even though it was only one street with twenty or so buildings, there was a general store, a barber shop, a bank, sheriff's office, hotel, some other businesses and of course a saloon.

Some of the buildings looked freshly painted while others were no more than a few unpainted boards slapped together. I rode right up to the livery stable. I dismounted, walked to the door, stood and watched a slender old man with wrinkles on top of wrinkles.

He took a red bandana out of his pocket and mopped his forehead with it. He stuck it back into his trousers and removed a plug of tobacco from his flannel shirt pocket. He took a big bite, placed the remaining plug back in his pocket. He chewed a couple of times and spit a stream of dark liquid out the door of the establishment, just missing me where I was standing.

"I'm sorry young feller. Didn't see you standing there. What kin I do for you?"

"I'm needing some information. I figured if anybody knows what goes on in town, it'd be the livery stable owner. You are the owner, aren't you?"

"Jubal Kincaid, ever since this town was a couple tents. What'd you wanna know?"

"Do you know Flanagan? Owns the Circle Four."

"Sure. I know Albert. Fine fellow. One of the best. Why you asking about him? You ain't gonna cause him no trouble, are you?"

"Just need to know if he was having trouble with anybody here in town?"

"Why would he? He's one of the most well-liked men in the county. Who are you and why you asking about him?"

"I'd like you to keep it to yourself, but Flanagan is dead."

"Dead! What happened?"

"That's what I'm trying to find out. My name's Yancy Calhoun. I'm Flanagan's silent partner. I found him shot and dying 'bout a month ago. He didn't live long enough to tell me anything. Do you know any of the men who worked for him? There's no sign of anybody living there for quite a spell. Also found some dead cattle. Been shot. Rest of the stock is missing."

"You know, now that I think on it, I ain't seen none of his crew in quite some time. Best place to ask is the saloon. Albert came into town every Saturday night just like clockwork. He was sweet on one of the girls there. Don't recall her name. Shouldn't be too hard to find out which one. Understand they ain't but three girls works there."

"Take care of my horse until I get back."

"Sure thing. And say, I'm real sorry 'bout Flanagan."

"See you shortly." I handed the reins to him, turned, crossed the street and walked into the Whistling Sparrow Saloon. It was dark and dank smelling of sweat, smoke and strong liquor. The saw dust floor was wet from spilled drinks. The bar was nothing but two hand sawn planks across a couple whisky barrels. The dusky room had four homemade wooden tables and matching chairs. The tables were empty. Two young ladies, looked to be in their early twenties, were standing at the end of the bar, each nursing a glass of dark liquid. More than likely tea or watered-down liquor. I walked over to the bar and looked at the bald-headed man standing behind it. He was short, barely one foot taller than the boards he was polishing with a dirty rag without any success His dark black eyes kept darting away from my face.

"What'll it be, stranger?" he asked.

"I'm looking for information." I answered.

"We don't have none of that here. Only drinks and female companionship. Now if you're interested in that I can help you, otherwise there's the door."

"You're a little testy, ain't you?"

"Just trying to run a business and mind my own business. Like I said. If you want a drink or a woman I can help. If not?"

"I know. Hit the road. Right?" He looked at me and nodded. I turned and faced the two girls. "You girls know any more than him? I can pay."

"Wait a minute, Mister!" exclaimed the bartender. They don't know nothing. You girls go on upstairs and don't be talking to this gentleman."

They started walking away, when one of them whispered as she passed me. "Out back. Ten minutes."

I nodded, tipped my hat to the bartender and walked through the door. As soon as I stepped onto the sidewalk, I turned down the alley to the back of the saloon. I hadn't stood long when the girl came out the back door.

She was the one who had whispered in my ear. "My names Marie. What was it you wanted to know cowboy?"

"I'm looking for information about Albert Flanagan."

"Why you asking about him?"

"He's a friend of mine. A real good friend."

"How do I know you ain't just pumping me for information and then you'll kill him?"

"Why would I want to kill him?"

"I'm just saying."

"Are you his girl?"

"Could be. Why?"

"Because Flanagan's dead."

"Oh no! I told him to be careful."

"What was he supposed to be careful about?"

"There was some men from out of state looking at his property. They told him there was a big possibility of gold being there. He was counting on it being true, 'cause he let his crew go. We was planning on getting married and going to go to California."

"Was there anybody else in town that knew about this?"

"Albert told everybody that would listen to him. I told him he needed to tone it down a little, but you know how he was?"

"Yeah, he always did like to brag when things were going good. Did anybody make threats against him?"

"No. He was very well liked here. You think somebody killed him for the gold that they ain't found yet?"

"People have been killed for a lot less. You can't think of anybody that didn't like him?"

"There was this one fellow. Owns the ranch next to the Circle Four. Name's Rudolf Finster. Him and Albert had words over who owned the rights to the creek dividing their land. I ain't never seen Albert so mad."

"When did this happen?"

"Day after Albert told everybody about the gold. You thinking Finster killed him?"

"I'm not drawing any conclusions yet. Just trying to put some facts together. I sure appreciate you talking to me. And I'm truly sorry for your loss. He was a good man."

She sniffed a few times, wiping her nose with a kerchief, turned and headed back inside. She turned at the door and said, "You could check with Sheriff McTavish. I know he'll help if he can. He's an honest man." She went inside, closing the door behind her.

I left the alley and walked across the street to the sheriff's office. I opened the door and saw a large, muscular man who looked as if he could handle any kind of trouble, except at the moment he was puking into a wooden bucket. I stood in the open door until he was done and stepped inside.

"Sorry 'bout that, stranger. As you can see I ain't doing too good. Come on in. I won't offer my hand 'case I'm contagious. I'm Jason McTavish. What can I do for you?"

"You sure you're up to answering a few questions?"

"We'll find out. What'd you want to know?"

"I'm asking for information about the confrontation between Flanagan and Finster. I understand it got pretty heated."

"What's your interest in this?"

"My name is Yancy Calhoun. Flanagan was my partner."

"What do you mean, was?"

"When I arrived at his place, I found him shot and dying. He didn't live long enough to tell me anything. I heard you could maybe help me."

"I know I had to break up that argument. I felt if I didn't, somebody was gonna get hurt bad."

"You know what it was about?"

"Most everybody knows what it was about. Finster wanted Flanagan to admit that he had full rights to the creek dividing their property. Excuse me please," he grabbed the bucket and disappeared into the back room. I heard him retching. He returned shortly wiping his mouth with his handkerchief.

"Maybe we better cut this short. I think I need to lie down on one of them bunks back there. There is one thing though. I got some flyers in yesterday's mail. One of them caught my eye. Two brothers. Jack and Jake Slawson. Wanted for murder."

"Lots of men wanted in these parts."

"Yeah, but these two were seen conversing with Finster a few days ago. I was planning on going after them until I came down with this croup. Flyer's on the desk. I've got to lay down. I'm sorry."

"You've been a lot of help. I hope you feel better real soon."

I shuffled through the papers on his desk until I found the one for the Slawsons.

"So long Sheriff," I hollered as I left the office.

I went back to the livery stable. Mr. Kincaid was shoveling out the stalls and rolling the wheelbarrow out the back door. He glanced up at me, nodded and kept going until he had dumped the load. He set the wheelbarrow down and came back inside.

"Find out anything?" he asked.

"You heard of the Slawson brothers? Jack and Jake. Might be working for Finster."

"Sure. I seen'em. Couple of rough customers, if I ever seen any. You say they may be working for Finster? Ain't no maybe 'bout it, he hired'em soon as they got to town. Didn't even let'em git a drink 'fore he sent off someplace. Come to think 'bout it, they did head off in the direction of Flanagan's place."

"You have any idea where they might be right now?"

"Finster's got a couple line shacks on both ends of his property, 'could be in one of them."

"Thanks, Mr. Kincaid. I appreciate all your help."

"Weren't nothing. Glad I could do it. Next time you see me, call me Jube. I'm too young to be called mister."

"I'll remember. So long."

The moon scurried behind a thick layer of dark clouds, but it was still light enough to see the corral. It was a hot July night and I pulled my bandana out of my pocket and mopped my face.

I saw a movement at the end of the corral. *Was it a horse or a person? If it was one of the Slawson brothers, then I was gonna have to change my plans.* The door to the cabin opened, casting a light across the corral. I could see clearly now. Both of the brothers were heading for their saddles. They were getting ready to leave. I wasn't going to let that happen. I lifted my carbine to my shoulder and pulled the hammer back. It made a loud clicking sound that caused the brothers to stop and look my direction.

"Alright boys, I got you covered. Don't try anything if you want to live to see the sun come up tomorrow."

They both hit the ground and rolled to the side. I let loose with a shot, more to let them know I meant business than to hit anybody. A bullet whistled by my head. I fell to the ground and crawled behind the water trough.

"Who are you stranger, and what do you want with us?"

"You the Slawson brothers?"

"Yeah, but we ain't done nothing wrong."

"I don't care to hear your sad story about being innocent. I got a flyer on the two of you. Dead or alive. I'm gonna take you in, either way."

"It's a mistake. That ain't us on that poster."

"We done had this conversation. You're going with me. How you go is up to you. Toss out your guns and we can keep you both alive."

They decided to stay alive. Two. 45s came flying out from where they were hiding.

"Okay, now, both of you come on out. If either one of you has another weapon, you're both dead."

They stood and stepped into the corral with their hands in the air.

"Don't shoot. We throwed our guns out yonder. We're unarmed."

CHAPTER NINE

Rebecca turned from watching Yancy ride out of sight. She went back inside and started to fold some clothes, when she noticed she wasn't wearing her gold locket.

She always wore it around her neck. She said her father had given it to her on her thirteenth birthday. It was her most prized possession and the only time she took it off was when she took a bath.

"I don't remember putting it back on last night. Where could it be?"

She searched the entire house and still couldn't find it. She walked into the kitchen and noticed there were several things missing. A loaf of bread, some sugar cookies and a few other things.

Am I losing my mind? I know those things were here yesterday. Well, worrying about them, isn't getting the work done.

She did a lot of work after eating a light lunch. It was getting close to dusk when she walked outside and thought she saw something moving in the barn door. She stepped back inside, grabbed the rifle and took off toward the barn with her finger on the hammer ready to cock it.

"Come on out, whoever you are. I know you're in there."

"Don't shoot! I'm coming out." A young girl stepped through the barn door. She was maybe nine or ten years old, wearing a too small dirty yellow dress. Her blonde hair was dirty and matted.

"I ain't done nothing. Why you want to shoot me?"

"I didn't know who was in there. What are you doing in my barn anyway?"

"I's just looking for a little somethin' to eat. I ain't had nothing since two or three days, but some bread I took from your house. I'll be going now, if you don't shoot me. You wouldn't shoot nobody in the back, would you?"

"I tell you what, why don't you come in the house with me? I think we can find something to eat. How's that sound?"

"Honest? You ain't kidding me?"

"Come on. I'm Rebecca. What's your name?"

"Susan Yvonne Brown. You can call me Suzzy. I'm ten. How old are you?"

"Ladies don't tell their age, but just between you and me, I'm older than you."

"That don't tell me nothing." They went inside and Rebecca set some crackers and cheese on the table.

"You want some milk with it?"

"That would be nice. Thank you, ma'am."

"You can call me Rebecca or Becky."

"I like Becky, so I'll call you that."

"Can you tell me what you were doing in my barn?"

"I got lost."

"How'd that happen?"

"I was traveling with my ma and pa. I went in the woods and when I got back the wagon was gone. I looked and looked, but I couldn't find them. I walked all day and night 'til I fell asleep. When I woke up, I saw this place and I hid in the barn."

"Did you stay in the barn all the time?"

"I did sneak into the house when you was taking a bath. I took this. I'm real sorry. It was so pretty I couldn't help it."

She held up Rebecca's gold locket. Rebecca reached and took it in her hand and pressed it to her heart, silently saying a prayer of thanks.

"How would you like to take a bath? I think I can find some clothes that you can wear."

"You mean in that tub you was in last night?"

"That's the one. You want to?"

"I'd like that. I ain't never had a bath before. Not in a big bathtub like yours."

"Come help carry water so we can heat it." They carried the water from the well, heating it on the stove.

"I think that's enough for now. You undress and I'll wash your back and your hair for you."

Suzzy pulled her dress over her head.

"Oh! Susan? Where? What happened to your back?"

"That's where my pa whups me. It don't hurt now."

"Where were you and your folks headed? Do you know?"

"Sure, we was going to Wisdom Rock, Texas. Pa said he was gonna work for somebody named Forster or Forset, somethin' like that. You gonna try to find 'em?"

"I'm not sure if I am or not. Let me wash your back for you."

She took the soap and a rag and gently rubbed the welts on little Suzzy's back.

"That feels real good. I could stay in this tub forever."

"If you did that you'd turn into a prune."

"I wouldn't neither."

"Come on, get out and dry off. I've got some old clothes here." She had gotten some of Flanagan's smaller clothes out of the closet.

"These are a man's clothes. I can't wear no man's clothes. "Case you ain't noticed, I'm a girl."

"And a very pretty one at that. It'll be alright until we can go to town and get you a real dress. Now put them on please."

She pulled them on and looked like a scarecrow.

"Use this belt to keep them from falling down."

"They do feel better than my dress. Thank you."

"You are very welcome. Are you ready to help me cook supper?"

"I used to help ma all the time when we still lived in a house, but that was a long time ago."

"Did your pa hit you often?"

"When I was little, he didn't never hit me. He only started hitting us when he lost his job and we had to move. Ma said he hit us to make hisself feel better. I don't mind if it makes him feel better."

"Oh my. You're such a sweet girl. You want to mix the batter for the biscuits?"

"I sure do." She took the bowl and started mixing the batter.

After eating, Rebecca asked, "you want to sleep in my bed tonight?"

"Where's your husband gonna sleep?"

"How do you know I've got a husband?"

"I saw him leave."

"Well, until he returns, you can sleep with me. Tomorrow I've got something to show you in the barn."

"I done seen'em if you're talking about the kittens?"

"How long were you in the barn?"

"Just a couple of nights."

"Let's go to bed now."

It was a restless night for them both. Suzzy kept tossing and turning all night, keeping Rebecca from getting any rest. She wasn't there when Rebecca reluctantly got out of bed. She dressed and went into the kitchen. Little Suzzy was breaking eggs into a skillet.

"Good morning, Becky. Did you have a restful night?"

"To be perfectly honest, no I didn't. Are you always so restless?"

"I don't know. Did I keep you awake? I'm sorry."

"Don't worry about it. Where did you get those eggs? I didn't know we had chickens."

"In the barn. That old rooster didn't like me coming in to get the eggs, but I convinced him it was alright."

"How did you do that?"

"I explained to him that the people who lived here really liked fried chicken for Sunday dinner."

"You are a very special young lady. I'm so glad you decided to sneak into my life."

CHAPTER TEN

It was an uneventful trip back to town with the Swansons. They were very cooperative, which surprised me.

"You boys work for Mr. Finster?"

"Not no more. We did a little job for him when we first come to town. He said he don't need nothing else."

"You mind telling me what little job it was you did for him?"

"He had somebody he wanted to put a scare into. We scared him alright."

"What did you do?"

"We rode up in front of his house and started pumping lead into the windows. I figure he got so scared that he run plumb to the next county."

"Did you go back later to check on the man?"

"Na. All Finster said to do was scare him. That's what we done. Why you asking all these questions?"

"That man that you shot at died in my arms. He was a real good friend of mine."

"We didn't kill nobody. We just shot through the windows."

"Did you ever think that he might be standing in one of those windows to see who was in his yard?"

"Mister. We sure didn't aim to hurt nobody. We might be bank robbers, but we ain't killers. We're awful sorry 'bout your friend. Does this mean we're gonna hang?"

"That's not for me to decide. But if I had my way, I'd shoot both of you and leave you for the varmints."

"But you ain't gonna do that, are you?"

"No. I'm taking you to jail so's you can stand trial. I will tell you this though. I don't have much hope for you."

"We didn't mean to do it."

"Yeah. I heard that already. How about let's ride the rest of the way without talking."

My insides were boiling, I was so mad. If Finster told them to only scare Flanagan, then there wasn't any way I could hold him responsible for his death. Unless I could convince the Swansons to tell things a little differently.

"What would think about not hanging?" I asked them.

"You really expect me to answer that? What'd we have to do?"

"I don't really blame you boys for Flanagan's death. I blame Finster. Now if someone was to say that Finster hired them to kill Flanagan, then he would be the responsible party."

"And this would keep our necks outa the noose?"

"I think I could convince the sheriff and a jury that you didn't mean to kill anybody. You'd have to go to prison, but you wouldn't have to hang."

"How's that sound, Jake?" he asked his brother.

"I'll agree to anything to stay off that scaffold," he answered

"Then we're agreed?"

"Agreed," they both said in unison.

The rest of the ride was quite with each of us thinking of how these two men had narrowly escaped the noose.

It was mid-morning when we arrived in front of the sheriff's office.

"Okay, boys, this is it. Climb down and let's check on accommodations for you."

We tied our horses to the hitching rail and went inside. The sheriff was sitting at his desk looking a lot better.

"I see you got'em. Have much trouble?"

"No. They weren't no trouble at all. They were very cooperative in more ways than one. How you feeling? You're looking better."

"I'm a lot better, but still not up to par. I'm feeling good enough to lock these gentlemen in a cell." He stood and motioned for them to head into the back room where the cells were located.

I heard him say, "You can bunk together or by yourself. Don't make no difference to me."

I heard the metal doors slam and the key turning in the lock.

The sheriff came back and sat down at his desk.

"Whew. Just that little bit tuckered me out. I sure appreciate you bringing them in. Did they confess to you? Did they kill Flanagan?"

"Yes, they admitted to shooting in his windows, but they didn't mean to kill nobody and I believe them."

"Don't make no difference whether they intended to kill or not, we got a dead man and they admit to shooting in his window. They'll surely hang."

"That's something I'd like to talk to you about. Finster hired these men to put a scare into Flanagan, but they did more than scare him. I feel Finster is responsible for his death. Now if someone were to say Finster told them to kill the man, then he could be arrested and held responsible."

"Yeah, I see where you're going with this, but you done said Finster only told them to scare him."

"If these boys could be sure of escaping the rope, maybe they heard Finster tell them he wanted Flanagan dead."

"I don't know. I've always prided myself in being an honest peace officer."

"What would be more honest than making the man responsible pay for the crime?"

"Alright, you've convinced me. Slawsons agree to this?"

"They said they'd do anything to keep from hanging."

"Okay, but I ain't feeling up to arresting him right yet."

"You could give me that honor."

"Raise your right hand."

"Why? I don't want to be no deputy."

"It was alright for you to go after the Slawsons, you had a flyer on them, but this time it needs to be completely legal, so's he don't wiggle out of it. If you want to do this, you need to be wearing a badge. Hold up your right hand."

Boy. This would make old Virgil turn over in his grave, Yancy Calhoun, a deputy sheriff.

"Here, pin this on. You're now a legally deputized officer of the law."

"Is it okay if I wait until tomorrow to go after him?"

"Sure. On your way, can you take their horses to the livery stable?"

"I'll do that. You get better. See you tomorrow."

"So long and be careful. You do realize that Finster might not want to come peaceable."

"I might enjoy that."

"Bring him in alive to stand trial, if you can."

I left the office, picking up the reins of the three horses, taking them to the livery stable.

Jubal was sitting on a stump in front of the building whittling on a piece of wood. He looked up and saw me crossing the street. I watched as he spat a long stream of liquid off to the side.

"Didn't come close to you that time. I see you got some extra mounts. They belong to the killers?"

"Yeah. Sheriff said bring'em to you."

"I reckon I need to try to sell the animals to help pay fer their legal fees."

"I don't think they're gonna need a lawyer. They're gonna plead guilty to a lesser charge of conspiracy."

"Conpir . . . what?"

"It means that they agreed when someone told them to kill Flanagan."

"Who'd they consp.. . . agree with? Finster?"

"Yes."

"I noticed you wearing a badge. That mean you're gonna arrest him?"

"That's what it means, after I go home and get a little rest. I'll be in tomorrow. See you then."

I grabbed the pommel, slipped my foot in the stirrup and pulled myself into the saddle.

"So long," he waved as I rode out of town.

CHAPTER ELEVEN

The warm summer air was thick with the smell of wildflowers covering the fields.

As I rode into the yard, I saw Rebecca and a small girl washing clothes in a cast iron pot over a fire. Rebecca didn't see me until the girl said something to her and pointed toward me.

Rebecca looked up from her work and saw me. She threw the wet clothes on the ground and ran to meet me. I reined up the horse just as she reached me. She grabbed my leg and held tight.

"Let me get down and give you a hug, gal?" I told her

"Oh, Yancy. You're here. You okay?" she asked.

"I'm fine, now let me get off this horse."

She let loose and stepped back. I slung my leg over and slid to the ground. My feet barely touched the dirt 'til she grabbed me around the neck. She looked up at me with those piercing blue eyes that caught me in a web of some kind, every time I looked into them.

I stood as if hypnotized, looking into them, when she said, "Well are you gonna kiss me?"

I leaned down and pressed my lips to hers. I didn't realize until that moment how much I had missed this. I felt like I had traveled a long way and I was finally home.

She increased the pressure on my lips promising of things to come.

She leaned back and looked at me. "I love you, Yancy Calhoun. And I missed you dearly. I'm so glad you're home. You are home, aren't you?"

"I'm home right now. That's all that matters."

I turned and looked at the little girl standing by the wash pot. "Who's your friend?"

"Come on. I'll introduce you," we walked arm in arm over to the girl.

"Suzzy, this is Yancy. Yancy, this is Suzzy. She's going to be staying with us for a while."

"Alright. I guess." I said hesitantly.

"I'm pleased to meet you Mr. Calhoun," Suzzy said.

"Call me Yancy." I told her.

"I knew you would like her. I knew it would be okay." Exclaimed Rebecca.

"We'll talk later." I said as I looked at her.

"Suzzy, can you hang the wash on the line while I get Yancy something to eat?"

"Sure, I can do that."

We walked to the house and went in the kitchen door.

"I suppose there's a reason why that little girl is here."

"Yes, there's a very good reason. You want a cup of coffee while I tell you?"

"Coffee would be good."

She told me the story of how Suzzy came to be at our place.

"I don't want to send her back to her parents for her father to beat her. I can't bear to think about that happening. Besides, they're probably in the next county by now. I can't believe they didn't look or her."

I started leading her toward the bed.

"Yancy, we can't. Suzzy might come in."

"Just one reason she can't stay."

"You mean you would let her go back to a father who beats her?"

"It really ain't none of our concern. A father has a right to correct his kid. Can't nobody get involved in family matters."

"Well I can! I will not let her go back to him!"

"You feel this strongly about it?"

"Absolutely. And I thought you would too."

"I want whatever you want." I told her.

"Then she can stay?"

"If that's what you want, then yes, she can stay, for a while."

"Thank you. Thank you. I love you so much more for doing this."

"How about showing me how much?"

"I'll show you tonight. That's a promise."

She kissed me with enough passion that I almost forgot about Suzzy.

"I need to get back out there and help her. I love you."

She pecked me on the cheek and hurried out the door.

"I'm coming, Suzzy." I heard her say.

What have I gotten myself into now? I thought. *I don't mind having a family, but not like this and not this fast. A couple is supposed to have some time together before having to put up with kids. But if it's true that I love Rebecca, then this is the way it's going to be.*

I poured myself another cup of coffee and sat at the table thinking to myself. When the cup was empty, I got up and went to take my horse to the barn. I removed the saddle gave him a good rubdown, then threw some hay in the trough.

I went back outside and stood watching the girls as they played with together. I will admit it looked like they were having fun, enjoying each other's company.

They started walking toward the house arm in arm. I followed close behind watching Rebecca as she swayed with each step. I could hardly wait for tonight when I would watch her slowly remove her clothes, then I would hold her nude body next to mine and touch her soft silky-smooth skin.

They both turned and stuck out their tongues at me, then took off running. I didn't try to overtake them. I calmly walked in the door.

"Suzzy baked the biscuits today. She did an excellent job. We'll have them with supper. Suzzy, you want to set the table?"

"Yes, ma'am."

"What is this ma'am stuff? I thought you were going to call me Becky?"

"Just being polite is all, Becky."

"That's better."

The meal was another great one. Rebecca was an excellent cook and I will say, the biscuits were very good.

"A fine meal, especially the biscuits. You did a real good job, Suzzy."

"Thank you, Yancy. It's okay to call you Yancy, ain't it?"

"I told you, you could. That is my name. Sure, it's okay."

"I'm real happy it was your place I found. I like it here."

"Let's see if you like it after you do the dishes?" Rebecca teased.

"I don't mind doing dishes as long as I can be here with the two of you," said Suzzy.

When the kitchen was clean and things put away, Rebecca said, "Suzzy, you'll have to sleep out here on the couch tonight."

"I know. You and Yancy got some time to make up for?"

"Suzzy! Let me get you a blanket for a cover."

She disappeared into the bedroom and came back carrying a blanket and a pillow.

"Here you are. Do you need to go to the outhouse before you go to bed?"

"I reckon I better." She went out the back door.

"She is very well mannered, don't you think, darling?" Rebecca asked.

"Yeah." I answered nonchalantly.

"Oh Yancy? You can't act as if you don't like her? I can see you do."

"Just get her settled in bed. I'm ready for bed myself."

Suzzy came back in hitching up her too big trousers.

"Tell Yancy goodnight. He's going on into bed."

"Goodnight Yancy. Thank you for letting me stay here with you and Becky."

"You're very welcome," as I felt a lump in my throat. "Goodnight." I stood, turned and entered the bedroom.

"Do you think he likes me?" I heard Suzzy ask Rebecca.

"Of course he likes you. Who wouldn't like you? Such a sweet girl. Now crawl under the blanket. Goodnight and sweet dreams."

"Goodnight Becky. I love you."

Rebecca came into the bedroom, wiping tears from her eyes. She looked at me and sniffed.

"Did you hear that? What she said?"

"I heard. Now come here." I held my arms open and she fell into them with her clothes on. Not the way I had it planned. Not at all.

We lay that way for a little while, then she got out of bed and started taking her clothes off. The lamp was turned down low, casting her shadow on the wall. Each article she removed caused my heart to beat just a little bit faster.

She was so beautiful and she was mine. I didn't want to have to share her with anybody, not even a ten-year-old little girl.

I watched that little heart shaped birthmark as it came closer to me. I kissed it and nuzzled my face as she lay beside me.

"I love you more than I can describe," she said.

"I love you too." I whispered.

"Oh Yancy! You've never told me that before. Do you really love me?" she asked.

"How could you doubt it?"

"Let me show you how much I love you?" she said.

Her hands and lips started to do all the familiar things and then some that weren't familiar.

When our passion had cooled, she lay with her head cradled on my shoulder.

"I have to go back to town in the morning."

"But you just came from town. Is it really necessary?"

"It is."

"Does it involve guns?"

"It might."

"Should I be worried?"

"I don't think so. I should be back before sundown."

"But what if you're not?"

"Then I'll be back as soon as I can."

"Goodnight my darling," she said.

"Goodnight."

Sleep and sex are wonderful rejuvenators. I woke the next morning to an empty bed, but feeling great. I looked through the window to a glorious morning sun.

I crawled out of bed and pulled my clothes on. I could hear the girls talking in the kitchen. I walked through the door and had to admit they were a couple of beautiful women standing at the stove.

They both had flour on the end of their noses. The smell of fresh biscuits filled the air.

"Smells delicious. Who's responsible for that?"

"We both have to claim that honor. Sit and I'll get a plate for you," said Rebecca.

She placed a platter with scrambled eggs, Johnnycakes, sausage and those fluffy hot biscuits with butter and a cup of maple syrup. It looked like a feast and tasted like it too.

"Ya'll gonna eat?" I asked around a mouthful of eggs.

"We ate earlier. This is all for you, because we love you."

I looked up from the food at the two of them standing with a silly grin plastered on their faces. And there was something else that I saw. A look that said they were telling the truth. *These beautiful females, one a small girl, the other a grown woman, both loved me.*

How could an old reprobate like Yancy Calhoun be so lucky? I knew deep inside that I surely didn't deserve it, but here I was wallowing in all this affection.

Now I have to go take care of this situation with Finster. I hope he comes peaceable. It hasn't been long since I wouldn't have worried about that. But since Rebecca happened to me, I'm just a little concerned about living.

Well, I need to get on the road. I wiped my mouth, pushed the chair back and stood up. I glanced at Rebecca. I could see the concern in her blue eyes.

"I'll be back before dark. Suzzy, you help Rebecca. I'll see both of you later.

I walked out the door and to the barn. I went inside and saddled my horse. I led him outside, climbed into the saddle, headed him toward town and we left the yard at a gallop. The sun was bright and warm on my face. I pulled the brim of my hat down for shade.

Last night kept running through my mind. *Did I really tell Rebecca that I loved her? Was that just lust or was it the truth?*

Why does life have to be so complicated?

I stopped in the sheriff's office. He was seated at his desk nursing a cup of coffee.

"Morning to you, Deputy Calhoun. I see you're ready to go. Want a cup of joe first?"

"Sounds good." I poured myself a cup and sat down in the chair in front of his desk.

"I figure I'll go with you this morning. I'll stay in the background and let you do the talking. But if he sees me, maybe he won't be as apt to cause any trouble. That okay with you?"

"You're the sheriff. Sure you want me to take the lead?"

"I figured you would want to, since Flanagan was your friend. Whichever way you want to do it is fine by me."

"If you're ready then, let's go."

He had his horse saddled and ready to ride, so we mounted up.

"I'll follow you." I told him.

We headed out the west end of town.

"How far is it, Sheriff?"

"Call me Jace. It's about 30, 35 miles. It's gonna be dark before we got there.

A crescent moon cast its silvery glow across the front yard of the house. It looked like a body in front of the house. We spurred the horses to a gallop rushing into the yard. There was a body lying on the ground. We stopped our mounts and jumped to the ground. I pulled my gun standing guard, while Jace checked the body for any sign of life.

"It's Finster. He's dead. See anybody?"

"No. Can you tell how long he's been dead?"

"Body's still warm. Ain't been long."

"That means the killer could still be here. You check the barn, I'll look in the house. Be careful." I told him.

I walked to the house, scanning the area for any type of movement. I reached the front door and twisted the knob pushing the door. It wouldn't budge. Something or someone was keeping it from opening.

I went to the window, trying to see inside, but it was too dark. I started to the back when I heard a shot. I took off running to the barn where the sheriff was supposed to have gone.

I showed as I rounded the corner. I didn't want to run into anyone with a weapon. I flattened myself against the barn wall.

"Jace, you okay?" He didn't answer. Jace?" Still no answer. "Whoever's in there needs to come out. I'm not in a very good mood and this ain't helping none. I'll give you 'til the count of three, then I'm coming in. I'll be shooting when I do. One, two, three! Here I come!"

I picked up a rock, put it in my hat and tossed it through the door. Three shots shredded the hat. I figured out where the shooter was hiding from those shots. I ran quickly to the opposite side right inside the door. I squeezed off a couple of shots in his direction. I heard a grunt from him. Maybe I got lucky.

"You hit?" I asked.

He answered with two more shots. I jumped across the floor to the other side. Now I was located right under the loft where he was. I was pretty sure he couldn't see me in this position.

"You realize this is going to end in only one way unless you give up."

Something wet landed on my hand. Blood. So I did hit him. All I have to do is wait him out. That blood leaking out is gonna make him weak.

"Last chance. Come on out, we'll take a look at that wound. Looks like you're losing a lot of blood. Wouldn't want you to bleed to death."

"Okay. I'm coming out. You're right, I'm bleeding pretty bad."

"I'm waiting. I wouldn't try nothing if I was you. Throw your gun down first."

A Colt .45 bounced on the ground.

"You got a rifle too. Toss it down."

A rifle landed beside the .45.

A bloodied leg stuck over the edge of the loft onto the ladder. The other leg followed. A large man wearing dungarees and a checkered shirt came down the ladder and stood on one leg said, "You wanna see 'bout stopping this blood?"

"Where's the sheriff?"

"He's in the back stall. I don't think he's hurt bad. He's lucky you showed when you did."

"You stay right there while I check on him."

"I don't feel like going no place." I held my gun on him as I walked to the back stall. I glanced inside and saw McTavish laying in the straw. He wasn't moving.

"Jace? You okay?"

He didn't answer. I looked at my prisoner and said, "I'm gonna step inside here and check the sheriff. My advice to you is not to move or you'll be bleeding in another place."

"Go ahead. I ain't going no place."

I stepped inside the stall and knelt beside the sheriff. I felt for a pulse. He was alive. I rolled him over on his back. There was blood on the side of his face. Looked like the slug creased his skull. *No telling how long he'll be unconscious.* I stood, walked back out.

"You gonna look at my leg now?"

"I'll get to it after I've taken care of the sheriff." I walked past him and out to the water trough. I wet my bandanna and went back inside. I carefully washed the sheriff's head. He mumbled something. I couldn't understand.

I've done all I can for him. The rest will be up to him and the good Lord.

I walked back out to the man leaning against the ladder.

"Alright, sit on the floor and I'll take a look."

He sat down hard, causing him to utter a loud grunt.

"Looks like it went all the way through. I got the blood slowed down in front, but I couldn't reach the back. I'm feeling kind of weak. Think I could have a drink of water?"

"Let me see 'bout this leg first, then I'll get a canteen. Turn over and lay on your belly."

He turned and spread out on the floor. I removed my pocketknife and cut a slit in his pants, then ripped them open so I could see the wound.

It was a pretty big hole where the bullet had exited. There wasn't but one way the stop the bleeding. That was to cauterize it, and if we took time to build a fire, it might be too late.

"You ain't gonna like what I got to tell you, but I've got to cauterize that hole. Only way to stop the blood."

"You do what you got to do. I don't think I can stay awake much longer. Everything's getting dim."

"Losing consciousness would be the best thing for you right now. You bite down on this piece of wood. This is gonna hurt like the fires of hell."

I twisted the lead out of the end of a .45 slug, poured the powder into the wound and lit it with a match. The flame flashed like a roman candle.

The man screamed like he was dying and then was silent. He had passed out.

I stood, went to my horse, opened the saddlebag and took out a small bottle of rotgut whiskey. I took it back and after taking a swing, poured it into the wound.

I untied his bandanna from his neck and wrapped it around his leg, covering the wound. I went back to the sheriff and took his handcuffs off his belt, went back to the man and handcuffed one hand to the ladder. Now I knew he wasn't going anyplace in case he got any ideas when he woke up.

I walked to the house and went around back. I reached for the knob when I heard some moaning coming from inside. I quickly opened the door and stepped through.

There, leaning against the front door was a woman. She was the reason I couldn't open the door earlier.

I rushed across the room and knelt beside her. I noticed she had been shot in the center of her chest.

Her eyes fluttered open and she cringed when she saw me.

"It's alright, ma'am. I'm a deputy sheriff. I'm here to help you. Can you tell me what happened?'

She mumbled incoherently. I stood, went to a bucket of water on the counter. I took the dipper and brought some back to her.

"Can you take a sip of water?" I held it to her lips and she opened them just a little and took a small drink.

I poured a little on my bandanna and wiped her forehead. She was sweating a lot.

She raised her hand and grabbed the dipper, pulling it to her lips.

"Okay. Let me help you?" I held it and she took another sip.

"Are you able to talk now?"

"You a deputy?"

"Yes, what happened here? What's your name?"

"I'm Mrs. Finster. Where's my husband?"

"Don't worry about him right now. Try to tell me what happened."

"Man rode into the yard, had words with Rudy, then shot him right there in the yard. Just shot him down like a dog. Is he alright?"

"How did you get shot?"

"I started out the door to help Rudy and the man turned his gun on me and the next thing I knew I was lying on the porch. I managed to pull myself inside and close the door. I'm hurt bad, ain't I?"

"If you're up to it, I'll take a look. I'm gonna have to remove the top of your dress. Is that alright?"

"I think you'll be wasting your time, but go ahead. Take a look."

I ripped her dress so I could see where the slug had entered her chest. She was lucky she had lasted this long. I pulled the torn cloth back over her and asked, "You want another drink?"

"I'm done for, ain't I?"

"I won't lie to you. Yes ma'am. I'm afraid there ain't nothing I can do. Maybe if I was a doctor, but I ain't. I'm real sorry. There is one thing you should know. I have the man that did this tied up out in the barn. I can promise you that he will hang for doing this."

"Hang him high." Those were her last words as her head slumped down on her chest. I found a blanket in the bedroom and covered her with it.

Now I need to talk to my prisoner and see if I can learn anything about what's going on. There's absolutely too many people dying.

CHAPTER TWELVE

Barton Norris was hired by the banker, Thomas Devlin, to eliminate all the people involved in his gold scheme.

"He wanted Flanagan's land because the railroad had said they would probably run their new track through his property. He created this sham about gold because he knew Finster and Flanagan would disagree about who owned the rights to the creek. When Flanagan was killed, he wanted Finster out of the way too. The woman was a mistake. She surprised me when she ran out the door. I ain't never shot no woman in my entire life."

"Well, you have now and you're gonna hang for it."

"You think they'd go easy on me if I told about Devlin's involvement in all this?"

"Maybe."

"Calhoun!" the sheriff was calling.

"I'm coming! You sit tight." I told Norris.

"How can I do anything cuffed to this ladder?"

I walked back to the stall where McTavish was leaning against the wall.

"Glad to see you awake. How you feeling?"

"Got one hell of a headache, but I think I'm gonna be okay. Did you get him?"

"I did. He's right outside."

"I'll be ready to take him in as soon as I can stand up."

"Don't push yourself. He ain't going no place 'til we do."

"I could use a drink of water."

"I'll get it." I stepped out, walked back to where I had set the canteen and picked it up.

"How' bout giving me a swig before you take it away?" asked Norris.

"I'll bring it back. Right now, the sheriff needs it more than you." I took it in, removed the cap and handed it to McTavish. He turned it up and drained it.

"I needed that." he said as he wiped his mouth with his sleeve.

"I'll try getting up if you'll give me a hand."

I grabbed his hand and pulled. He struggled to his feet still holding on to me. He reached and steadied himself on the wall of the stall, releasing my hand. He rubbed his head with his empty hand.

"I'll be alright if I can just stand here for a minute. Go ahead and get the horses. I'll be ready by then." I walked past Norris and headed toward the horses.

"Hey. Where's that water?" asked Norris.

"You can have some on the way to town. I ain't gonna let you die of thirst. Where's your horse?"

"Out behind the house." I got his horse, leading it back and picked up the sheriff's and my horse.

I went back in the barn and found McTavish unconscious on the floor. I rushed inside and checked his pulse. I didn't feel anything. I rolled him over and put my face close to his nose. Nothing. He was dead. Another mark against Norris and the banker Devlin.

I took a horse blanket from the stall next door and covered his body.

I went back to Norris. "Okay, let's go."

"What about the sheriff?" he asked.

I didn't answer. I took the cuffs from the ladder and said, "Give me your other hand."

"You don't have to do that. I ain't gonna try nothing. Sheriff didn't make it, huh?"

"I'm not in a very good mood, so if I was you, I'd just do what I was told without any discussion. Think you can do that?"

He put his hand out and let me put the cuff on it.

"I'll leave them in front so you can ride, but I'm gonna be watching you close. Come on, mount up. Let's get started."

"I don't know if I can ride with this bum leg."

"I think you'll be able to suffer through it, if you try real hard."

80

CHAPTER THIRTEEN

It was morning, with the sun shining a bright yellow hue on the horizon, when we got back to town.

As we rode past the bank, Devlin was standing in the doorway. When he saw Norris, he ran back inside, slamming the door.

"Don't look like he's very happy to see me," said Norris.

"I'll take care of him as soon as you're locked up."

We stopped in front of the jail.

"I never was too fond of being locked in a cell."

"You won't be in it long. As soon as we can hold a trial, you be leaving."

"That ain't funny."

We tied the horses in front of the jail and went inside.

"Well hello, Deputy. Did you bring us some company?" asked the oldest Slawson, Jake.

I ignored him.

"Pick one out," I told Norris.

"This one will work." He walked inside, turned and pulled the door closed. "You gonna take these things off now?"

He turned his hands sideways and stuck them through the bars.

"I'll just lock this first." I turned the key hearing the click as the lock slid into place, then I took the cuffs off his wrists.

"Make yourself comfortable, I'll see if I can locate a doctor for your leg."

"You mean you ain't no doctor? I wouldn't a let you work on it if I'd knowed that."

"How come you're being so nice to him? Is he somebody special?" asked Jake.

Again, I ignored him. I stepped on the sidewalk and watched as the town came to life. Folks scurrying back and forth getting ready for the day.

I noticed Devlin talking to a group of men. It looked like a heated discussion. He was talking and pointing toward the jail. The men were acting agitated.

One of them grabbed a rope off a nearby horse and started waving it in the air. It hadn't taken long for Devlin to stir up trouble.

I stepped back inside and crossed the room to the rifle rack. It was locked. I went to the desk and started rummaging for the key. I found it, along with a bottle of whisky, in the bottom drawer. I picked up the bottle, twisted the lid off and took a long drink.

"Boy, did I need that." I set the bottle down and picked up the key, unlocked the chain on the rack and grabbed a double barrel shotgun. I loaded both barrels and stuck a couple shells in my pocket.

I slugged down a couple of swallows of the whiskey. It burned all the way down, hitting my empty stomach with a vengeance.

Probably didn't need that on an empty belly.

I walked out the door just as the group of men were almost to the jail. I held the shotgun in the crook of my arm.

"You boys can stop right there," I shouted.

"Who are you?" One of them asked.

"This badge should answer that question. Can I help you with something?" I asked calmly.

"You can step aside. We're gonna string Norris up," the leader said.

"Why would you want'a do that?"

"'Cause he killed Finster."

"Who said he killed Finster" I asked.

"Mr. Devlin told us. Finster was a good man. We aim to lynch Norris for killing him."

"How did Devlin find out about Finster being dead? I hadn't told anybody about it. Think about it a minute. This only happened last night. I just now locked Norris in a cell. How could Devlin know about all this unless he hired Norris to kill Finster?" I explained. "Could be you're hanging the wrong man."

"Where is Devlin? Someone shouted.

The men started looking around.

"He ain't here. Come on, let's find him. He's got some questions to answer. The men scattered, trying to locate the banker.

A horse came racing out the door of the livery stable with Devlin in the saddle.

"There he is," someone yelled. "Let's get him."

The men ran for their horses and took off after him. Didn't look as if I was going to have to worry about him.

I went inside, broke open the shotgun, removed the shells and put it back in the rack.

"Sounds like you saved my hide. Thanks."

"You didn't escape the rope. You'll still hang."

"Ain't the same thing as a lynching. I seen a few of those and I don't want no part of a pack throwing a rope over a limb."

"You're welcome," I said.

I left the jail taking the horses across to the stable.

Jubal was sitting in front whittling.

"Looks like you talked your way outa that one. You headed home now?"

"Yes. Is there somebody in town can watch over the prisoner? A mayor or somebody important?"

"Ain't I important enough?"

"Thought you didn't get involved?"

"I can handle a little somethin' like this. At least 'til you get back."

"Thanks. See you a little later. Here's Norris' horse. Oh, I almost forgot. Is there a doctor in town?"

"Sure is. Doc Watson. You need him for something?"

"Yeah. Prisoners got a hole in his leg. I patched it best I could, but he orta have a doctor check it."

"You go ahead, I'll go get the doc. Don't you worry about nothing. I'm capable of taking care of everything. So long."

One last thing, get some men to head out to Finster's place and pick up the three bodies."

"How come three?"

"Finster's wife is in the house."

"Damn! That's a shame. I hope the prisoner tries to escape. I sure would like to plug him."

"That's what we got laws for. I'm sure he's gonna hang. So long, and thanks."

I climbed into the saddle and pointed my horse in the direction of home. *I sure liked the sound of that. Home.*

As the sun disappeared from the sky the stars began peeking out, then the darker it got, it seemed like there were thousands of stars dotting the sky. It was a beautiful sight.

The darkness was so quiet, I didn't hear anything but the horse's hooves on the hard packed earth and the jingling of the harness along with the creaking saddle. There was an occasional sound of some night birds in the distance.

I wonder how Rebecca's going to react when I got there. I told her I would return before dark day before yesterday. What is that up ahead? A man leading his horse, no, it's a mule. He looks like a prospector.

He held up his hand when he got closer.

"You heading that direction, are you?"

"Yeah, I'm headed home."

"A little girl and a growed woman live with you?"

"Yes, why?"

"Woman's bad sick. Got a bad fever. The girl asked me to get the doctor from town. I'd been there already if'n this damn mule hadn't throwed a shoe. You better hurry home."

"You take my horse and bring the doctor back here lickety split. I'll take your mule and go on home. Can you do that for me?"

"I'll ride like the wind. Be back soon I can."

He hopped up on the horse with more energy that I would have thought he had. He spurred the animal and they galloped toward town.

I picked up the mule's reins and began the trek home. No matter how hard I pulled or how much I cussed, the mule only had one speed.

CHAPTER FOURTEEN

We reached the yard almost an hour later. I dropped the reins and ran the rest of the way to the house. I busted through the door and into the bedroom. Rebecca was in the bed. Suzzy was wiping her face with a damp cloth. Rebecca didn't look good at all. Sweat was running down her face and her once glowing skin was washed out and very pale.

Suzzy looked up and saw me.

"Oh Yancy, I'm so glad you're here. Rebecca has been calling for you."

I went to the other side of the bed and knelt down. I took her small hand in mine.

"I'm here, Darling. It's Yancy. I'm here. Can you hear me?"

I felt a gentle squeeze on my hand.

"She heard me, Suzzy. Has she had any water?"

"She wouldn't take none."

"She's got to have liquid to fight the fever. Go bring some water in here."

She went out and came back carrying a bucket of water. "You try to get her to drink some water and I'll go fix some tea."

I went into the kitchen and located a tin of sassafras tea. I boiled some in a pot, poured a cup full and carried it back in the bedroom.

I put my hand behind Rebecca's head and lifted it so she could swallow.

"Open your mouth and try to take some of this."

She took a little, coughing a little bit.

"Take some more, sweetheart."

She drank all of it. I laid her head back on the pillow. She mumbled something. I placed my head close to her lips.

"I love you," she whispered.

"I love you," I said, meaning it with all my heart and soul. I did love her and I wanted to spend the rest of my life with her. "I'll be right back," I squeezed her hand. "Suzzy. You keep bathing her face with that wet cloth," I went back into the kitchen.

She needs some food in her stomach. What can I fix that will build up her strength? Jerky. I'll make a broth with beef jerky.

I searched the entire kitchen and didn't find any jerky. *Where can it be? My saddlebags.*

I ran out the door and remembered that I didn't have my horse. The old timer had taken it to town.

"Dammit! Dammit! Think! What kind of broth can I make?"

I went back in the kitchen and opened the cabinet doors. There on the shelf were rows of jars of canned goods. *She needs a broth of some kind, preferably some kind of meat. Chicken. I'll kill a chicken.*

I ran outside looking for the chicken pen. I searched the entire area. No chickens. I turned to head back in the house, when out of the corner of my eye I saw a rabbit scurrying out of the corral. I drew and shot in one fluid movement. The rabbit was tossed in the air with the impact of the bullet. I had my meat for a broth.

I hurriedly skinned and cleaned the animal and rushed back into the house.

I cut it into small pieces and boiled it in a pot. As it thickened, I dipped out some in a cup, grabbed a spoon and took it in to Rebecca.

Suzzy was faithfully dabbing her face with the damp cloth.

"Let's see if she will drink some of this?" I set the cup on the small table at the edge of the bed. I knelt down and propped her head up with the pillows. I dipped out a spoonful and held it to her lips.

"Open up, Darling, this is going to make you better."

She took the entire cup, but she was exhausted from the effort. Her eyes opened and she gave me that hypnotizing look that always leaves me tongue-tied.

I took her hand in mine and gently squeezed. "I'm right here, Sweetheart, I'm not going anyplace."

I felt her squeeze back and her eyes closed.

"Have you eaten anything?" I asked Suzzy.

"I ate a couple of crackers and some cheese. "

"Come on, let's get something to eat."

I was hungry myself and sleepy. I hadn't slept in two days and I was exhausted.

We went into the kitchen and looked around.

"There's some rabbit left. You like rabbit?"

She shook her head.

"Look in that cupboard and grab a jar of something to go with fried rabbit." I proceeded to stoke the fire and finished cutting up the rabbit.

"Is green beans okay?" she asked.

"Anything you want is fine. Come on over here and empty them into this pan."

"I can't open it. It's too tight."

"Give it to me." I twisted the lid off and handed it back to her. She dumped the ingredients into a small pot and set it on the back of the stove. There was beginning to be a nice aroma of food cooking.

"I'm sure glad you're home, Yancy."

"Me too. I am very glad to be home."

The meager meal was delicious. Suzzy and I polished it off in no time at all. We were both licking our fingers when we heard a buggy pulling up in the front yard.

I jumped up from the table and rushed outside. The old timer was stepping out of the buggy and reached to help an elderly man get out.

"I brung him, just like I said I would. This here's Doc Watson. He's a mite old, but he's a real good doctor. How's the lady?"

"Give me my cane and stop your jawing. Get outa my way," exclaimed the doctor.

He rushed past me without any hesitation and went inside the house.

"You look all tuckered out, mister. When's the last time you had any sleep?" the old timer asked.

"I'll get some when he says Rebecca's gonna be alright. Not before."

"You cain't do her no good if'n you git sick too. Why don't you lay down on the couch and jest rest your eyes? I'll tell you what the doc says when he's looked at her."

"I believe I'll take you up on that. You wake me as soon as he has a report."

"I will. Now go."

I lay down on the couch and the minute my head hit the cushion, I was out. I don't know how long it was, but I felt somebody poking my shoulder.

"Yancy. Yancy!"

"Go away. Leave me be."

"Yancy! The doctor wants to talk to you."

I was immediately awake.

"I'm awake. How is she Doc? Is she gonna be alright?"

"She's gonna be fine. I found a tick in her hair. Her fever broke a few hours ago. She's asking for you."

"Thanks Doc." I rushed through the door and Rebecca was sitting up with a smile on her face.

"Oh, Yancy. You are here. I thought I was dreaming. But you are here."

"I'm here and I'll be here as long as you want me."

The doctor came in the room. "You had a mighty close call, young lady. If this young man hadn't gotten that liquid in you, well, it's a good thing he did. I'm gonna have to head back to town. It seems a certain banker had an accident and needs stitches. I was working on him when Roger told me what was happening out here. I told Devlin to just sit still until I got back."

"What happened to him? Do you know?"

"It seems he was running from some men chasing him, when his horse bolted and he was thrown to the ground landing on the back of his head. He's a very lucky man. That fall could have killed him."

"I thought those men were chasing him to lynch him?"

"I don't know anything about that. I only know when they brought him in, he was bleeding profusely. The men said something about the hostler, Jubal Kincaid told them to bring him to my office. I gotta go now. You get a lot of rest, young lady."

"So long and thank you so much, Doctor."

He turned and went out the door.

Suzzy came in and asked, "You need anything, Becky?"

"I need you to come over here and give me a hug. The doctor told me you were the one who kept my fever down with the cold water. Thank you."

"I just glad you're alright. I was really worried. Did you know Yancy could cook?"

"Really? Maybe he can help in the kitchen from now on."

"I only cook in emergencies. Besides, I can't bake biscuits as good as yours, Miss Suzzy," I teased.

"Well, I think someone needs to fix something for the sick woman," said Rebecca.

Suzzy and I both jumped up and almost knocked one another down as we scrambled out the door.

"Grab a couple more of those jars and let's fix a feast for our <u>sick woman</u>."
"You want me to whip up a batch of biscuits?"

"That sounds great. Do your magic, while I scramble some eggs. Say, where did these eggs come from? I looked and couldn't find any chickens."

"They run wild. They lay their eggs in the barn. I gather about four or five eggs each morning. Eggs is what makes the biscuits so fluffy, didn't you know that?"

"I did not know that. That's good information to have."

"Hello! In the house. Anybody in there?" It was the old timer sticking his head in the doorway.

"Come on in, join us for a meal. That is if I can get this girl to start whipping that batter."

"I really need to get on the trail. I been out in the barn tightening the old mule's shoe. It was just loose. I also took the saddle off your horse and gave him some hay. That's a real good animal you got there. You treat him good and he'll treat you the same. Now I must bid you farewell. I'm shore glad your misses is gonna be okay. You've got a fine family here. Maybe I'll see you along the trail again. Goodbye to you."

"Goodbye." He closed the door.

"He was a funny man," said Suzzy.

"He might be funny, but he probably saved Rebecca life. Now you need to start stirring if we're gonna have them fluffy biscuits."

"Right away, Captain."

"What's going on out there?" we heard Rebecca.

"Nothing!" We both answered.

I peeled some potatoes and sliced them for frying. It was a simple meal, but a nourishing one. Scrambled eggs, seasoned potatoes and fluffy biscuits.

"I'm going to take some of this in to Rebbeca," I told Suzzy.

I dished up some on a plate and took it in.

"It looks delicious. Did Suzzy bake the biscuits?"

"She did, but I did the rest. Does it look delicious too?"

"Yes, it does and I do believe I'm hungry. Will you sit with me while I eat?"

"I'll sit here as long as you want me to."

"I was really worried when you didn't come back by dark. And then I started to feel sick. The next thing I knew was I was in bed and Suzzy was bathing my face with a wet cloth. I don't know why I got sick."

"The doctor told me you had tick fever. Once he removed the tick you started getting better."

"Where in the world did I get a tick?"

"Don't worry about it. You're alright now. That's what matters. You want me to feed you?"

"I think I can manage, but thank you. I would like a kiss before I start though."

"I think I can manage that." I leaned down and kissed her on the lips.

"I don't think I would have gotten better if you hadn't come home."

"Let's just think about you getting better, so you can get up and do this cooking and housework."

"Oh, you're so mean, but I love you anyway." She took a bite of her food. "Hmm. It is good."

I sat there beside her and watched as she took a bite, chewed, swallowed, then the same thing again and again until the plate was empty.

"Thank you so much. I needed that. Now I'm feeling a little tired. Tell Suzzy to come in and I'll tell her goodnight."

I took the plate from her and went into the kitchen.

"Suzzy had her head down on the table fast asleep. I picked her up and laid her on the couch, covering her with a blanket.

I went back to tell Rebecca and she was asleep. I pulled the covers up around her neck, kissed her on the forehead and went back out.

I took one look at all the dirty dishes and decided I needed some fresh air. I stepped through the front door and marveled at the beautiful sky. I went back inside and brought a chair out and sat on the porch.

I looked at the night sky, saw a shooting star.

I quickly made a wish before it died out.

"I wish that Rebecca makes a full recovery. I wish that Suzzy doesn't have to go back with an abusive father. I wish that everything would be perfect from now on. Okay. Maybe that's pushing it a little too far, but it doesn't hurt to wish."

I leaned back in the chair and thought to myself.

That old prospector said I had a nice family and you know, he was right. I do have a wonderful family. Should I ask Rebecca to marry me and make everything legal? Or should I just leave things the way they are? Yancy. Why do you always doubt yourself? You know you love the two of them. Why not show them by asking her? I'll do it first thing in the morning. When Rebecca is up to it, we'll go into town and talk to somebody about Suzzy living with us permanently.

Now that was settled in my mind, I went back inside to face those dirty dishes.

EPILOGUE

When Rebecca recovered fully, the three of them took a trip to town where Yancy and Rebecca were married in the church. They asked the pastor about the legal ramifications of keeping Suzzy. He explained that since her parents had made no effort in locating her, it seemed feasible that she continue living with them.

They stopped in Mrs. Hamilton's Mercantile and bought clothes for Suzzy and Rebecca. Rudy still had eyes for Rebecca.

On the way out of town Suzzy made the statement, "That Rudy is kind of cute,"

When they arrived home, Suzzy asked Yancy and the new Mrs. Calhoun if they would come to the barn.

"Please don't tell me we've got more cats?" moaned Yancy.

Other Books by J.C. Hulsey

Angel Falls, Texas

Velvet Sky, Arizona

Angry Orchard, Colorado

Clear Stone, Wyoming

Itching Tree, Idaho

Windy Butte, New Mexico

Devil's Dance, Dakota Territory

Redemption Road

Red Rose

The Concho Kid

GUTSHOT
The Old Man

The Pistol Preacher

******

Some Stuff I Wrote

Some More Stuff I Wrote

Even More Stuff I Wrote

Newest Stuff I Wrote

Brand New Stuff I Wrote

Brand Spanking New Stuff I Wrote

Look What I Found

Oldest Coon Hunter in Somervell Co

(Compiled by)

Confessions of a Battered Wife

(Compiled by)

www.ingramcontent.com/pod-product-compliance
Lightning Source LLC
Chambersburg PA
CBHW071335140726

47996CB00005B/1993